The following stories are not recommended for children or anyone who is currently:

- ❖ breastfeeding
- ❖ swallowing lemonade
- ❖ delivering bad news
- ❖ attending a funeral
- ❖ plotting revenge
- ❖ stroking a baboon

The laughter you are about to experience will make it impossible to perform any of these tasks in a dignified manner.

The Department of Deceased Dragons

STORIES FROM ANOTHER UNIVERSE

Daniel Brewster

THE DEPARTMENT OF DECEASED DRAGONS
Copyright © 2022 Daniel Brewster

All rights reserved; no part of this publication may be reproduced, distributed, or transmitted in any form or by any means, including photocopying, recording, or other electronic or mechanical methods, without the prior written permission of the author, except in the case of brief quotations embodied in critical reviews and certain other non-commercial uses permitted by copyright law. For permission, write to the author

This is a work of fiction. Any references to historical events, real people, or real places are used fictitiously. Otherwise, names, characters, and places are products of the author's imagination

Written by Daniel Brewster
Cover design by Daniel Brewster (using Adobe Express)
In-book images for title page and chapters from Flaticon.com

ISBN 979 8 215 77267 6

www.books2read.com/danielbrewster

Contents

Santa Roo and Kanga Claus 1

Shape-shifty 25

Magical Properties 33

Pouncing Shadows 55

The Sea Climber 66

Literary Friction 71

How to Win Friends and Save the World 83

Don't Shoot the Messenger—He's Already Dead 94

Stay Tuned or Suffer the Consequences 100

For all the dragons that didn't make it.

SANTA ROO AND KANGA CLAUS

The only true Christmas story.

– Chapter 1 –

One night, when Australia was asleep, a kangaroo saw a glimmer on the horizon.

A shiny red sleigh glided down from the stars, pulled by eight reindeer slaves, exhausted and wheezing from their travels. Their master, a pudding-shaped man with a jolly red coat and a fuzzy white cloud on his chin, yanked on the reigns. The lead reindeer's nose began blinking red, signalling it was time for Master's toilet break to the others.

The kangaroo watched in wonder as the shimmering sleigh slid to a halt across the dark orange sand.

'Oh, for fuck's sake, Blitzen!' boomed the obese man, standing up. 'How many times have I told you to let Cupid land first! You're gonna get us all killed!'

The kangaroo noticed all the reindeer shuddering at the sound of their master's voice. They nervously eyed the blustering, sweaty-faced behemoth as he stumbled out of the sleigh and waddled over to some foliage.

'Who is he?' the kangaroo whispered.

As the man pulled down his pants and urinated against an unwilling shrub, the kangaroo noticed a large red sack sitting in the sleigh, with a glittery-green box poking out the top. It had a gold ribbon tied around it.

Hopping closer, the kangaroo saw that the sleigh was full of many bags of all sizes, not dissimilar in look and feel to the pouches of his mother and auntie and all the other lady-roos of his clan.

'Psst.'

The kangaroo looked around, startled. The obese tyrant was still spraying his acid-yellow torrent all over the poor shrub, whose leaves were now hissing in a cloud of steam.

'Who said that?' he whispered.

'Over here,' came a voice.

The kangaroo turned to the reindeer and realised they were staring at him—at the tip of his tail, in fact.

The one at the front, with the glowing red nose, opened its mouth and spoke. 'Hurry, there's little time.'

Amazed, the kangaroo hopped over as silently as it could. 'You can speak?'

'Yes, we all can,' replied the red-nosed reindeer. 'Your kind and ours were once relatives, long ago. Before the Age of Wrongful Magic thrust us apart.'

'The Age of Wrongful Magic?'

'Yes, but I'll explain that later. First, I need you to find the blue pouch in Santa's sleigh.'

'Santa?' asked the kangaroo, looking back at the man, who groaned with relief as a new surge of liquid, possibly from a second bowel, inundated the shrub's withering branches. 'That's his name?'

'Listen, fuck face,' snapped the reindeer. 'Are you gonna help us or not?'

The kangaroo hadn't been spoken to so harshly since it accidentally burned down a forest as a wee-joey. But it immediately saw the look of regret on the reindeer's face.

'I—look, I'm sorry. We're just in a rough spot right now. Have been for a long time.'

The kangaroo saw the lines of pain and misery etched on each of their faces. The scars of many hopeless winters. He knew he had to do something.

'Blue pouch, right?'

'Right,' nodded the reindeer. 'And bring it here, quick as you can.'

The kangaroo hopped to the sleigh and rummaged amongst the pouches with its snout. There were pouches of every colour under the sun: purple pouches, emerald pouches, golden pouches, silver pouches; pouches made of plastic, pouches made of cotton, pouches so fantastic, pouches that were rotten, pouches with aromas, pouches with no scent, pouches doubled over, pouches merely bent, pouches—

'What the fuck?!' snapped the red-nosed reindeer under his breath. 'Hurry up, there's only one blue pouch; it's right there!'

Ah, thought the kangaroo. So it is.

It took the blue pouch in its claws and hopped back to the reindeer.

'The name's Rudolph, by the way,' the reindeer said. 'But you can call me Rudy.'

'Oh, uh,' said the kangaroo, 'Pleasure to meet you. I'm Nameless. You can just call me that.'

The reindeer all shared a look.

'Nameless?' said Rudolph. 'Who on Earth called you that?'

'My mother,' said Nameless. 'She said I couldn't have a name anymore. Not after I...'

The reindeer, selfless and noble, regarded the kangaroo with compassion. 'Well, Nameless,' said Rudolph. 'As long as you're with us, you're gonna have a name. And by Jove, it's gonna be worth the effort of giving you one.'

The kangaroo felt a strange feeling deep in its chest, something it hadn't felt since before he burnt the forest down and was disowned by his clan: acceptance.

'I hereby name you Hopper. Saviour of Christmas.'

The reindeer nodded in agreement, for it was the perfect name, and this kangaroo was indeed a saviour, though an unlikely one.

'I—I'm the saviour of... What did you call it?'

'Christmas, boy!' exclaimed Rudolph. 'Surely you've heard of Christmas, haven't you?'

Hopper, as he was now known, had never heard of such a thing. He had never seen such wonderful creatures as these and had never, in all his 12 years in this dry and desolate land of his, seen a horrid, greasy man wear a red suit with so many stains.

'No. No, I haven't. But it was worth the wait if it meant meeting all of you.'

The reindeer were moved by his words, but Donner thought of something the others had not.

'We neglected to ask you, dear Hopper. What are your personal pronouns?'

'Oh,' said Hopper, shuffling nervously. 'He/him is fine. I've always felt comfortable with that.'

Donner smiled. 'He/him it is,' he said. 'He/him it is.'

Rudolph, more socially conservative than most reindeer, concealed an eye roll as best he could. 'Okay, well, now we've got that out of the fucking way, perhaps we can focus on ending our slavery—or would you like to check his sexual orientation?'

'Well, now that you mention it—' began Donner eagerly until Blitzen shrieked.

'He's coming!'

Hopper turned and saw that Santa was pulling his pants back up, with great difficulty but also with tremendous vigour.

'Quick,' said Rudolph. 'Open the pouch, and pour the dust on my nose.' Without hesitation, Hopper did so and saw that the dust was no ordinary dust. It did not make Rudolph sneeze, and it did not look dry. In fact, it looked like a million tiny stars floating down like raindrops in a dream. (Editor's note: No one, including the author, knows what that means.)

'*Calla fhurende,*' Rudolph began, swaying side to side. '*Calla memendo, orbitras callas risendo.*' His fellow reindeer joined in, swaying in unison and speaking the strange words as an echo. Hopper watched in awe as the magic dust melted, turning Rudolph's nose light from red to blue.

'Ohh, you bastards!' came a deep, grating voice. Hopper saw Santa running towards him with murder in his eyes. 'You're dead! You're all fucking dead!'

– Chapter 2 –

Did I mention Santa swears a lot?

– Chapter 3 –

The reindeer completed their chant. A great chain of lightning whipped down from the sky and wrapped itself around Santa, forming a cage. Santa dared not touch any part of his electrified prison lest he burst like a moth against a bug zapper.

'What have you done?!' he cried. His beard grazed one of the electric bars, burning the tip in a puff of smoke.

Blitzen stood tall and proud. 'How d'ya like that, ya fat fuck?!'

'Blitzen!' scolded Donner, never imagining Blitzen would utter such words.

Hopper was in shock.

'Quickly!' barked Rudolph. 'Untie us!'

Uncertain of what was happening, Hopper obeyed, carefully pulling on the leather straps binding each reindeer to the other.

One by one, the reindeer leapt away from the sleigh, freedom surging through their legs. They bounded about, leaping up high and spinning in the air.

'You did it!' cried Dancer. 'You saved us!'

'Hopper, you're our hero!' cried Dasher. 'You absolute legend!'

Hopper didn't know what to say.

Blitzen and Comet ran over to Santa and began spitting on him. Over and over, they barraged him with one vindictive spray after another.

'Piece of shit!' cried Comet. 'What's it like to be treated like nothing, huh?'

Santa began moaning and weeping, unable to evade the onslaught of saliva and grass shoots. He was trapped, inches away from death by electrocution.

Hopper was disturbed by the indignity of their actions but felt unsure about speaking up. 'U-Um,' he finally said. 'Is this really justice?'

Rudolph watched mercilessly, his glassy, snow-globe eyes glinting with a spark of vengeance. 'Let him suffer for a while,' he said coolly. 'Let him know the taste of his own malice.'

As the cage crackled and wobbled with energy, the reindeer finally relented. Blitzen had accidentally bitten his own lip, making his last seven or eight spits bloody.

'Alright!' Santa cried out, wiping the muck from his eyes. 'Mercy! I beg for mercy!'

The other reindeer watched silently, no longer bounding for joy, no longer kicking the air. They simply watched from a position of power over their former master, a power they had long dreamt of but never thought would be theirs.

'Any of you! Mercy! Y-You can't leave me locked in here forever!'

'Get the magenta pouch,' said Rudolph, not looking away from the pathetic sight before him. The others smiled, knowing what he had in mind.

Except for Hopper. 'What's in the magenta pouch?' he asked nervously.

Rudolph shifted his gaze to the innocent kangaroo. 'It's just as I told you,' he said with a cunning smile. 'You're the saviour of Christmas.'

As Comet trotted back from the sleigh with the magenta pouch in his mouth, Hopper wondered what all of this meant.

'Wait a second,' he implored. 'Can someone tell me what's about to happen?'

The reindeer were silent. Comet passed the pouch to Rudolph with a knowing look.

'Everything will soon make sense,' said Rudolph. As he was still speaking, mighty thunder pounded the dark horizon. Hopper saw an enormous eye opening and closing between the two brightest stars. He nearly fell backward, but his trusty tail kept him steady.

'W-What was that?!'

'What was what?' said Comet, looking at Hopper, then at the horizon. There was nothing but the night and its constellations. 'Hopper?'

'Y-You didn't see it?'

The reindeer grew concerned.

'See what?' asked Rudolph.

Santa peered at them through the bars, his menacing grin aglow with the blue aura of his lightning cage. 'Ohh, *I* saw it, kangaroo,' he teased. 'Do you know what that was?'

Dasher kicked a mound of dirt at Santa, most of it sizzling against the electrified bars. 'Quiet, you!'

Santa held his smile.

'Hopper,' he continued, 'Would you call what you saw a blink or a wink?'

'Impossible,' gasped Rudolph, dropping the magenta pouch. 'The Eyes of Destruction—they're just a fairy tale!'

'No,' Santa laughed. 'I'm afraid not.'

The other reindeer all looked at Rudolph.

'Rudy?' said Prancer, lips quivering. 'What do we do?'

Rudolph dropped his gaze for a long moment. He knew, deep down, that his darkest fears were about to become a reality.

'There's nothing you can do, foolish beast,' mocked Santa. The reindeer's faces were plastered with defeat. 'And as for me… I must depart.'

Rudolph immediately buried his snout in the magenta pouch, coating his blue nose in pink magic.

'Enjoy the end of the world,' Santa cackled. 'Ta taa!'

'No!' cried Rudolph, leaping forward with his new, shiny pink nose—but it was too late. Santa vanished in a flash.

- Signal lost -

>//: INCOMING TRANSMISSION...
>//: MESSAGE RECEIVED. DECRYPTING...
>//: PLAYING MESSAGE...

URGENT MESSAGE FROM NORTH POLE
From: Head Elf, Sebastian Rodbury (Dimension 7)
To: Head Elf, Gildeberry Rothchild (Dimension 8)
11:47 pm GMT, December 25, 2049

*Santa safely recovered.
Reindeer traitors left behind.
Magic of Christmas 98% absorbed.
Eyes of Destruction activated.
Request permission to enter Dimension 8.*

RE: URGENT MESSAGE FROM NORTH POLE
△:84 pm GMT, December 25, 64∮

*Well done, Sebastian.
Come on through.
That was quick.
Only 500 years.
Expect a bonus from Management.*

Shame about the livestock.

>//: END TRANSMISSION

– Chapter 4 –

Hopper stood silently amongst the reindeer, frightened and confused. He looked at the horizon every so often to see if that gigantic eye would reappear, though he dreaded seeing it again.

The empty, electric cage buzzed wildly for a moment before flickering out of existence. The air was tense, and Hopper could stand it no longer.

'I don't know what's happening or what all of this means,' he blurted out. 'But I didn't live through abandonment, and years of pain and loneliness, only to find you wonderful, magical creatures and throw it all away in despair. There must be something we can do. Something to… save Christmas.'

Rudolph lifted his heavy gaze and regarded Hopper with newfound respect. But it was all for nothing.

'What you say is admirable. But there are things at work here you know nothing about. Forces so great, even a thousand reindeer could not hope to withstand them.'

Hopper jumped over to Rudolph and picked up the magenta pouch, now empty. 'Here,' he said, tapping the pink light of Rudolph's nose. 'What does this do?'

Rudolph didn't see the point in explaining. In fact, the glow of his nose was slowly fading the more despondent he became.

'Rudy,' insisted Hopper, gently lifting his chin. 'Don't give up. Not yet.'

With a sigh, Rudolph mustered the will to speak. 'It's pure magic,' he said. 'Unlike what they manufacture at the North Pole. Found in Nature.'

'Well, what does it do?'

Rudolph looked at the other reindeer, who were beginning to lie down in defeat. Dasher looked away, holding back tears. He had suffered longer than all the others, being the eldest.

'I was hoping to use it on Santa. To neutralise him.'

'Neutralise?'

'After hundreds of years of using magic—synthetic magic—his system is drenched with impurities. Sneezing on him with this nose would have removed his ability to absorb any more magic from the world. It would have made him powerless.'

'So,' said Hopper, trying to understand, 'You're saying Santa was stealing the magic from our world?'

'Correct.'

'But why?'

Rudolph sat on his hindquarters and looked out at the moon. 'It's what they do. The Christmas Syndicate. They operate across the multiverse with impunity. Stealing magic wherever they can. Twisting it to their own ends.'

'The multi... what?'

'The multiverse. An infinite set of universes of unending variety. Essentially, every manifestation of every possible combination of particles and subatomic particles.'

Hopper had to sit on *his* hindquarters after hearing this, as all these new ideas were making his head spin.

'In other words,' said Rudolph, 'Access to unlimited power. And the freedom to use it, as they have for over a hundred thousand years, to control the lives of every living creature that exists, or ever will exist.'

Hopper gulped. These ideas were so complex and frightening to him that they began to unsettle his stomach. Just as he was about to let a pint of sewage loose on the earth, he held his nerve and found a dash of courage in his beautiful beating heart. This would be too much for an ordinary kangaroo, he thought. But he didn't want to be an ordinary kangaroo.

'Rudy,' he said, clenching the pouch in his paw. 'You said I was going to save Christmas. How, exactly?'

'It's too late now,' said Blitzen, turning over on his side. 'Santa's gone. We can't give you his Essence.'

Hopper looked at Rudolph, confused. Rudolph took a weary breath before responding. 'Once his power was rendered inert, we were going to extract his magical essence and place it in you.'

Hopper didn't know what to ask next.

'Because,' added Donner, 'We thought you were the Santa Roo. Foretold by the Reindeer Sages, long ago.'

Before Hopper could say anything, Cupid chimed in. 'That symbol on your tail we were gawking at earlier. It's the Flame of Christmas. It appears in the oldest prophetic manuscripts.'

'Th—this?' said Hopper, inspecting the tip of his tail. He saw a familiar shape in the discolouring of his fur, which he had seen every day since he was a joey. 'I thought it was just a birthmark.'

'Turns out you were right,' muttered Dasher, flicking a stone with his front hoof. 'The prophecy was a crock of shit.'

Hopper took a moment to process everything he'd heard. He knew how crazy it all sounded, but he'd also seen real magic this night. That alone, he thought, should be enough to change any kangaroo's perspective on what's possible in the world. And what of the prophecy? How slim were the chances of him crossing paths with Santa and his reindeer—in the most isolated part of the world—and having a mysterious mark on his tail that looked like this 'Flame of Christmas'? Surely this all meant the prophecy might still come true. Didn't it?

With the wind gusts rising from the east and moonlit storm clouds in their wake, he settled on one final question. But it was not a question for Rudolph or the other reindeer. It was a question for himself. One he had been asking for over a decade without ever being able to answer: one that might save Christmas.

'How did I burn the forest down?'

The reindeer looked at Hopper, bemused.

'He's gone loopy,' said Dasher, drawing shapes in the dirt with his antlers. But Hopper was lost in his own world of thought.

'It rained that morning,' he continued, hopping slowly. 'The trees, the plants... they were damp.'

Rudolph tilted his head, intrigued.

'I was hopping between Mother and Auntie. They were whistling.'

'Whistling, you say?' said Rudolph, standing up. But Hopper's mind was still in the past.

'I felt cold. So I...'

By now, all the reindeer, even Dasher, were hooked by his story.

'I imagined fire.'

Rudolph, walking closer, thought he could see the reflection of flames in Hopper's eyes as he spoke.

'And suddenly, there was one.'

Only now did Hopper realise he had been the centre of everyone's attention.

'You mean,' said Comet, 'You thought it, and it happened?'

'Yes, I... I guess it did.'

Cupid lifted his front hoof and pointed it at Hopper. 'Why are you only remembering this now?'

The reindeer all waited for an answer, but Hopper didn't have one.

'Trauma,' said Rudolph, wisely. 'Knowing you had the potential for such damage and destruction, at such a young age, you buried it. Deep within your memories. Beneath the scars of your psyche.'

Rudolph's every word rang true to Hopper.

'But… Why did I remember the fire at all? Why did I let myself remember the banishment, my Mother, my Auntie?'

'Because you were ashamed,' said Donner. 'You felt you deserved to suffer, so you let yourself remember just enough to bring you pain.'

A wave of sympathy rippled through the reindeer, who all looked at Hopper with soulful eyes. Donner walked over and gently rested the underside of his head on Hopper's neck. 'It wasn't your fault, sweet Hopper. You are not to blame.'

Hopper dropped his head and held back tears as the other reindeer came to his side and comforted him.

Rudolph looked up at the stars through watery eyes and knew that hope shone down upon them through the darkness.

– Chapter 5 –

In the years that followed, long after the reindeer taught Hopper how to harness the mighty ways of magic, and long after they defeated the Christmas Syndicate and poked out the Eyes of Destruction with righteous incantations; long after they captured and imprisoned Santa, and reverted him to his true, evil form as a withered, grey, bitter kangaroo known as Kanga Claus. When the trees of the Australian landscape were unshackled from Wrongful Magic and restored to lush and vibrant frondescence. When the snow fell gently across the barren deserts once more, bringing life, colour and beauty from ancient times past—when murky brown waters found their lustre again in crystal blues and glimmering streams of aqua. When the dinosaurs returned and used their strength and skill to build homes for lost and wayward creatures, from every coastline to every mountain height, and all the land was rejuvenated through the restoration of Rightful Magic—after all this—Hopper was at peace.

He wore the Crown of Christmas every year, glistening with starlight, spreading joy and hope across the globe.

But most precious to him were his friends. All eight of them antlered, unbound, and free to fly without whip or strap. They circled the world with him each year for over four centuries, to strange and distant lands, spreading love and magic to every willing creature, great and small. It brought him such joy and fulfilment that he could hardly believe it.

But it was all real; it was pure magic. And Hopper knew he was the Santa Roo.

SHAPE-SHIFTY

When a shapeshifter can no longer change himself, he changes the world.

Close the door. Sit down. I gotta tell you something. I'm not an ordinary man. Sure, I like TV. Eating. Sleeping. All the normal things. But one thing makes me stand out from most. I'm a shapeshifter.

That's right. You heard me. I can become whatever I want, whenever I want. A coat hanger? Sure. A fridge? No problem. A smartphone? Well, that's a little harder. But the point is, I can be just about any*one* or any*thing*.

I could be George Clooney from the 90s. Frank Sinatra in his prime. Hell, I could be Big Bird if I really wanted. Right now, I'm some guy I saw in a book store a couple of years back. He was nice to me. I like seeing him from time to time. Hearing his voice makes me feel calm…

Hey hey, relax, would you? I'm trying to tell a story here. I promise I'll answer anything you want. Just… Oh, this? It's not loaded. It's just something I like to carry around. To feel safer. I got jumped six months back when I tried out a face I saw in a magazine. Some gal from Sweden, I think. I wanted to know what it felt like to have those cheekbones. Shouldn't have done it at 11pm in the park. Big mistake.

Now, where was I? Oh yeah. I have a gift. But it comes at a price. The more times I change, the uglier my true face becomes. I've done it so many times now I can't stand looking in the mirror. I deliberately fog up the glass a little before I shave, just enough so I don't see all the scars and wrinkles.

And no one can help me. No doctors. No surgeons. I'm on my own.

No, no, don't mistake me for one of those split personality types. I haven't got multiple voices rattling around in my head. It's just me. The hero with a thousand faces, as Joseph Campbell might say. Except I ain't a hero. I'm just a bum trying to make his way through life. An uneducated, unread bum.

I *could* be a hero if I really wanted, I guess. But why risk the danger? What do I get out of it? I'm guessing you don't like me that much after hearing that. But ask yourself: would you risk your life every day to save a bunch of strangers? I mean, really? What about *your* life? What about what *you* want?

Hey, no need to flinch. I said it's not loaded. If I put it down here, will that make you feel more comfortable? Okay, there. It's not gonna jump off the table.

What is this, eighteenth century? This must be some kind of storage room for antiques. The guy who owns this place is richer than I thought.

Damn it, where was I? Oh yeah. *Life.* Maybe you want to find someone you can settle down with. Start a family. Own a house. Buy a moose, I don't know. If I threw my hat in the ring to be a hero, taking out criminals and running into burning buildings, I'd be dead within a month.

Do you know the mortality rate for superheroes in this town? Eighty-five per cent. That's right. Eighty-five. Most of them die within 18 months of putting on a cape. No one tells you that. All you see in the papers is how great everything is. I know, right? Used to be that the news only told stories about people dying and suffering. But once people started getting powers, all that changed. It became the best money-making, uh—*narrative*, I think they call it. People started getting excited to read the news. Like they were living inside an action movie. But what about all the heroes that didn't make it back in one piece?

What about Ned the Nuke? Remember him? That's right, the guy in the yellow spandex. Used to be famous up until two years ago when all those journalists memory-holed him the night he got mauled to death at a shipping yard. Yup, I knew it! I can see it on your face—you never heard about that. He just slipped out of the public's consciousness, like he never existed. Happens all the time. Those jerks over at the Times did a number on you, that's for sure. They're not just writers; they're magicians. They make people look at one hand while they pocket something with the other.

Remember that huge fight between Black Tiger and Fish Oil? That's right. *The exact* same night, the police were zipping a body bag over poor Ned's face. The whole thing was orchestrated. What are the odds they'd have a massive fight and end it with a marriage proposal? That's reality TV is what it is. They do this all the time. Meanwhile, some poor bastard was probably crushed beneath his camper trailer in that mudslide outside town while those two *fakes* were putting on a show for the cameras.

Poor Ned. He never was good around dogs.

Hey, are you comfortable? I could find you a cushion or something. I don't really know what else is in here. I could take a look if you... No?

Okay. Suit yourself. I thought your type'd want something a bit fancier. Guess you just want this all to be over. I don't blame you. I've wanted that for a long time.

Well, if you hear me out, I promise you'll be back sipping cocktails with your pals in no time. I just need you to listen. I got something to say that no one's been willing to hear. But I figure you're the type of person who's a bit more open-minded. I saw you on the news the other day after that Grout Girl incident. You were asking questions no one else has asked for years. I noticed. Especially when they cut you off and went back to the newsroom. You reminded me of those real journalists that went extinct right around the time all these superheroes started popping up…

Hey, answer me this: why do so many fake heroes have animal names? Did their PR guy work at a zoo or something? They really oughtta diversify. Kind of gives the game away. Is that a smile? I knew it; you're not like the others. Or maybe I'm making you nervous. Sorry about that. I know. I promise I won't take much more of your time.

So… So what was I saying… Oh yeah. Being a superhero. I'm saying that no one should ask me to jump on the superhero bandwagon when it's halfway down the cliff. All that'll happen is I'll get my name in the paper for saving one or two people, then I'll die by stepping on some half-rotten staircase in a basement, snap my neck and get forgotten like the rest of them.

Meanwhile, the ones that never die, the fakes, will keep doing their pretend battles, making millions with some new line of shaving cream or bullshit fragrance. They'll do just fine. But I'll be dead.

You know, this mansion used to be owned by Remote Man. Do you remember him? The first superhero back in the 80s? All he could do was change the channel by clicking his fingers. Scored himself a sweet deal with that big TV company over in Okinawa. Lucky bastard. I think he sold it to Mr Mermaid before he moved into a retirement home. You should talk to him. He knows what I'm...

Oh, he is? Damn. I... I didn't know that...

Is that... You always carry a notepad, huh? Well. Now I'm sure I picked the right person.

And you really can stop worrying about this. It's not even a real gun, just a cigarette lighter. See, watch this. There. Now, why don't I just skip ahead to the reason I'm here? I want to tell you a story. A real story. One that'll break this facade right open for all to see. It'll either win you an award or get you fired.

But the way I see it, if you want history to see you as a real journalist, it's gotta be one or the other.

MAGICAL PROPERTIES

Disclaimer: No Penguin Classics were harmed in the making of this story.

– Not All Witches Are Bitches –

That's just mindless prejudice. For instance, take Helena Gobtrot. She put herself through university working two jobs, babysitting the neighbour's kids every second Thursday, feeding old Mrs Carmoodle's cat, volunteering at the homeless shelter on study breaks, and donating blood once a month. Noble acts of service for her community, all the while knowing that same community would burn her at the stake if it ever found out she was a witch. That's character.

'Have you ever worked in real estate, Ms Gobtrot?'

The job interview was going well, as far as Helena could tell. Mr Kemperstein, the man sitting across the table—dark suit, red tie, opal cufflinks—seemed genuine and welcoming. While each of his questions had been fairly standard, he asked them with an expression that said, 'Gosh, you're great.' Then again, that might have just been in Helena's head. She couldn't be sure. Unless she sneakily cast a mind-reading spell... No, she swore she wouldn't cheat. She was too honest for that.

'Um, yes,' she began, 'I helped my uncle sell his, uh, mansion not too long ago.'

'A mansion?' said Mr Kemperstein with great intrigue. 'That must have been quite the learning experience.'

More than he knew. In fact, it was a haunted castle.

'Yes,' said Helena. 'I oversaw everything from photos to marketing, open house inspections, and finally, the auction.'

Mr Kemperstein leaned forward. 'And what did it sell for, if you don't mind me asking?'

'One-point-eight million.'

'Skittles and marshmallows!' he blurted. 'Oh, I'm sorry, I—' Face blushing, he didn't know how to apologise for his outburst. Meanwhile, Helena wondered how red he would have gone if she revealed it was sold to Dracula's least favourite nephew.

Mr Kemperstein regained a semblance of dignity as he straightened already-straightened papers and adjusted his cufflinks. Then, with a sober expression, he looked Helena directly in the eye. 'When can you start?'

– The Witch's Sister Had a Big Ol' Blister –

Magdalone, Helena's bratty older sibling, was waiting for her when she got home.

Helena had been beaming all the way from the job interview at the real estate agency. Until she saw her sister waiting on the porch.

'Help me, Helena!' she whined, as she always did, selfish and pathetic. 'My blister's back! Pop it for me! Pop it now!'

Helena sighed as she stepped through the doorway of her small, greying house. Magdalone followed, slamming the door behind her as she often did when she didn't get her way and dropped to the floor.

'You said you'd help me whenever I got a blister!' she bellowed.

'No,' Helena said through gritted teeth, 'I said a *doctor* can help you, seeing as you're too lazy to learn the basics of skin care.'

'I don't want a doctor!' Magdalone whinged, 'I want *you* to do it!'

'Kill me now,' said Helena under her breath. A half-second later, a grotesque statue, perched above her shoe box, reached for her neck with its claws.

'Just a figure of speech, Bartholomew! Down!'

The grotesque returned to its blank-faced pose, no longer desiring to kill her. Helena was such a powerful witch that mere casual utterances could be spells. It was something she had to be wary of.

As she walked across the black and pink chequered tiles into the grand atrium, she saw her pet eagle, Kirk, swoop overhead from the ninth floor down to the greenhouse on the eighth.

In case you hadn't noticed, her home was a magical mansion. On the outside, it looked like any other house on the street. But on the inside, it held wonders and marvels beyond imagining. Ten floors high, with enormous rooms and winding corridors, secret panels and mysterious objects from other worlds... This was Helena's sanctuary.

Unlike her sister, she was not only a powerful witch but an imaginative one. And magic without imagination, as her father used to say, is at best boring and, at worst, dangerous. Helena did her best to keep Magdalone away from the general public for its own safety. Part of that strategy was to build this grand house, with the help of her magical imagination, to keep Magdalone as busy and entertained as possible.

While Helena was proud of what she had built, she also felt a hint of regret. A feeling that Otherlings like herself deserved a home just as much as her. But instead, a significant number of them lived in squalor and fear. Werewolves, phantoms, ghouls, fiends, ogres, wood demons, writers. All hiding from society, afraid to show their faces or participate, unable to make the world a better place. If only the world would accept their kind, they could earn a living like anyone else and get off the streets.

'Oh no, it's gone all gooey! And it's all your fault!'

Helena sighed and marched over to her miserable sister, who was cross-eyed, looking at the pimple on her forehead.

'Hold still,' Helena said, tilting her sister's head back.

It was a big one, alright. Pimples are the most common ailments for witches, especially those who spend their days thinking the world is to blame for all their problems.

'What did you do this time?' Helena asked.

'Nothing!' squealed Magdalone, screwing up her stupid face. 'All I did was tweet about organ donors and how selfish they are!'

As Helena began rubbing her fingers to cast a spell, she couldn't help but feel her sister was a hopeless tragedy.

'You really are a k'arphutz, aren't you?' (That's a witch's insult from the old tongue, which I shan't be translating for all our sakes).

'I'm your older sister; you don't get to talk to me like—ow!!'

The pimple popped out of existence in a puff of green smoke.

'There,' said Helena, dusting her hands. 'Good as new.'

Then, a rhinoceros burst through the front windows, tumbling across the tiles in a cacophony of blood and glass.

– The Witch's Riches Paid for Stitches –

Oh, dear. What a mess. What a bloody, awful mess.

That was what Helena thought, hours into the clean-up, looking down from the first-floor bannister at two-dozen bucketfuls of blood clinking with shards of glass.

Her hand was almost entirely stitched up. The tip of the beast's horn had gashed it open when it barrelled past.

'Who was that, sister,' asked Magdalone, licking a rainbow lollipop twice the size of her face.

'It was a morphling, Erbert Nearodome, who lived down by the old factory.'

Magdalone tried to put her mouth over as much of the lollipop as she could.

'Nhever hheard of hhim,' she said, drooling.

'Don't be disgusting,' Helena said.

'I chan't hhelp it!'

The poor man occupied Helena's thoughts all night, long after the rhino carcass and its innards were thoroughly cleaned up and the front windows were magically restored.

'It's just so unfair,' she said at dinner. 'Transfiguration is a dangerous art. He didn't know what he was doing. He had no one to teach him.'

'Mm, yes, indeed,' said Kirk the eagle, sitting opposite her. He held a slice of garlic bread aloft—'A tragedy if I ever heard one.'—before taking a ravenous bite.

'I just don't know what to do,' Helena continued, staring deep into the gravy bowl by the potatoes. 'I want to help, but I feel so… Powerless.'

'Well,' began Kirk, dabbing his beak with a napkin, 'I suppose you could start with a thorough examination of your priorities.'

Helena was taken aback by this remark.

'My priorities?'

'Quite,' he said, lifting a glass of red. 'You say you're powerless, yet you are the most *powerful* witch in all the land. If anybody can help these poor wretches, it's you.'

Helena had nothing to say in response.

Kirk took a powerful sip, his beak chattering against the rim. He savoured every drop and tossed the empty glass onto the floor, smashing it to pieces.

Helena leaned back in her chair. 'Are you saying I should quit my new job? I earned it through honest, hard work, without any help from magic.'

'No, my dear,' said Kirk, tilting his head almost entirely to one side. 'I'm saying you haven't been honest with yourself about what you really want in life.'

Helena's first reaction was to feel offended. But then, after remembering Kirk had an eagle eye for people's blind spots, she relented. Since she left home at seventeen, Helena had always felt unsure which direction would lead her to her true self. Stabbing a head of broccoli with her fork, she glided it through the peas on her plate like a ship voyaging through the ocean. A ship lost at sea.

After a silence, Kirk found his moment to speak again, delicately. 'Perhaps there's a way to make a difference in this world *and* fulfil your life's dream.'

Helena knew she wanted to help people like her find the right house. Somewhere they could call home. A place they could feel safe and free to be their true selves. But the world wasn't made for Otherlings. Only a few of them could adapt to human houses. The lucky few.

But what if... No. That couldn't possibly work. Could it? As an idea took form and became a real possibility, Helena looked up from her plate at Kirk. She saw his wise eyes peering back at her. She couldn't believe how lucky she was to have a bird like him as a friend. 'Kirk,' she said, shaking her head with a smile. 'No one helps me see things differently better than you.'

Kirk smiled. 'Being me,' he said, turning his head upside down to peck a bean on his plate, 'That comes with the territory.'

Helena laughed. As she munched on her scrumptious dinner, thinking through the details of her plan, Kirk felt the need to say one last thing before clearing his plate and going for his evening flight. 'I'm proud of you, you know. For getting that job.'

Helena knew. But it warmed her heart all the more to hear him say it.

– The Witch's Snitches Gathered in Glitches –

Helena was nervous about the Zoom meeting. The attendees were her seven best contacts in the bay area for the goings-on of Otherlings. For her plan to work, she needed to know the demographics of creatures living in each region. But with so many of her kind living poor and transient lives, this was something she couldn't do alone.

That's why she needed her *Snitches*, as she playfully called them. They were cursed or transmogrified in some way, as all Otherlings are. But these seven, in particular, were the heart of the community. They organised clothes swaps, soup kitchens, social work services, and health seminars. No matter where you fell on the demonic–angelic spectrum, you knew one of these seven creatures had your back.

'I think you're on mute,' said Merkidon the Mummy through his muffling bandages. 'I can't hear anything.'

Cynthia the Siren emerged from her pool in the top corner of Helena's screen. 'That's because your head's wrapped in five layers of cloth, and your ears are over two-thousand years old!'

As more of Helena's Snitches slowly made their way into the Zoom call, Helena could see she was having internet troubles. The screen froze from time to time or became awfully pixelated.

'Walter,' she said to the wraith in the bottom left corner, 'Are you sucking on the 4G again?'

'No, not me,' he said, holding a steaming cup of tea up to his shadowy face. 'Promise.'

'Probably those bloody banshees,' moaned Cynthia the Siren. 'They fly over the city this time every Thursday, revving their vocal cords, disturbing the waters.'

Helena could see the group was already growing impatient, so she decided to press on and hope for the best.

'Okay, Snitches, thank you all for coming,' she began. Each monstrous creature looked squarely at their respective webcam. They may have been a rowdy bunch by nature, but they had enough respect for Helena to listen quietly.

'I called tonight's meeting to share an idea I've been mulling over for the past few weeks.'

Malloneous Mudman, the giant mound of slippery wet sludge, straightened his glasses every so often as they slid down his face.

'As you know, I recently got a job as a real estate agent. I've been there for three weeks.'

She looked past her computer screen and saw Kirk walk into the room. He gave a gentle wave of his wing as if to say, *don't mind me*.

'But as much as I love helping people find the perfect home, there'll always be a hole in my heart for those of our kind living on the streets.'

Transporto the Third, a man constantly zipping across the world against his will, managed to remain in front of his computer long enough to hear this. 'Yes, but—' he said, before vanishing with a little pop, then reappearing half a second later. This continued as he spoke. 'There's a reason so many of us can't live in a regular home, what with <*pop! ... chzip!*> unique requirements that aren't easily <*pop! ... chzip!*> impossible to live in a human house without causing massive problems for neighbours and <*pop! ... chzip!*> I mean, just look what happened to Danny's Den of Wolves last Summer.'

Catching the gist of what he said, the group nodded in agreement.

'I'm forced to agree with Transporto,' came a voice from Polodius, a motionless demonic statue. 'I mean, look at me. Whenever I want a midnight snack, I can't walk from the bedroom to the kitchen without scraping the walls with my wings. The plaster's damn-near destroyed. It's ridiculous!'

Helena's Snitches broke into a vigorous discussion about the finer points of living as an Otherling in a world made for humans: the brightness of light bulbs, the fragility of bathroom tiles, the blandness of box-shaped rooms, the lowness of ceilings for the flight-inclined.

It was an intergenerational problem that no one had been able to solve for decades. Helena knew that if she didn't take control of this, things would go the way they always went: a downward spiral of complaining and woe-is-me until everyone found themselves back where they started, with absolutely no way forward.

While this was happening, Kirk had climbed onto Helena's armchair in the corner and snuggled himself down on a mound of soft blankets.

'Okay, okay!' said Helena, firmly. The chatter of the group died down. 'We all know how hard it is to live in this world. None of us forgets the nightmare of helping Malloneous Mudman move house last year.'

The group remembered soberly.

'Who needs twenty-seven bath tubs?' muttered Merkidon the Mummy.

Helena continued. 'But we must think outside the box if we want a better future for our community.'

'What do you propose?' asked Transporto.

Helena leaned forward. 'As you know, my family's magic forbids anyone living with me, except blood relations or familiars.'

The group nodded.

'That's not your fault, Helena,' said Cynthia the Siren. 'There's no way around the ancient laws of old magic.'

'I know,' said Helena. 'Which is why I've devised a way to use *new* magic. My magic. To help people like us.'

Walter the Wraith tilted his shadowy face in curiosity.

'I propose,' Helena continued, 'That we use my family's fortune to buy all fifty houses currently for sale across the bay area. With my new job as a real estate agent, I'll have early access to each owner and the ability to make deals before any of them go to auction.'

Malloneous Mudman scratched his dripping chin. 'That's incredibly generous of you, Helena. But it's not illegal, is it? We'd hate for you to get in trouble.'

'Not in the slightest,' she replied. 'I checked with my boss, Mr Kemperstein. Though he was quite perplexed when I asked him.'

Kirk chuckled.

'But I have to move quickly,' she continued, dreading her next words: 'Darmon is returning.'

Everyone shuddered at the sound of that name.

'Darmon!' gasped Transporto before popping away.

'I thought he was dead!' shrieked Cynthia the Siren, slapping her water with rage.

Kirk jumped off the armchair and flapped over to the computer desk, blowing crumpled post-it notes everywhere as he landed. 'I'm afraid it's true,' he said, peering into the webcam. 'My spies in the north confirmed it this morning. He's very much alive. And he'll be in town within a matter of days.'

Silence rippled across the screen. They had all believed that Darmon perished in the Black Fire ten years ago. On that great and terrible night when the world's most powerful wizards stormed Vile Manor and put an end to his injustices once and for all.

Or so they thought.

'But the Elders sacrificed themselves to destroy him,' said Walter the Wraith.

'I was there,' added Merkidon the Mummy. 'For all nine hours of the battle. I saw them die. All of them. Including Darmon.'

'Those were dark days,' said Polodius, the demonic statue, face downcast. He had once allied himself with Darmon, believing the dark magician would liberate him from his stone prison. But it was just a lie. And the things Polodius had done to his fellow Otherlings in the service of that terrible master haunted him to this day.

'Don't beat yourself up, old chap,' said Walter the Wraith. 'Those days are long gone. We know you're one of us, now.'

'*Are* they long gone?' said Cynthia the Siren. 'If Darmon is back, what else will follow?'

'History does tend to repeat itself,' said Merkidon the Mummy.

Helena exchanged a knowing glance with Kirk. They knew this bombshell would never be taken well by the group. Nevertheless, she wasn't going to let it ruin her good plans.

'I... I understand how shocking this news is. But it's all the more reason to enact my plan as soon as possible.'

The group looked at their screens half-bemused. Helena explained.

'Darmon recruits people with false promises. Those who are desperate. Those who are destitute.'

'One moment, dear,' said Malloneous Mudman. 'How does buying ordinary houses for Otherlings solve their problems?'

'This is the key to my plan,' she said, eyes wide open. 'I intend to create a secret mansion inside each one. With new magic. Custom made to suit each resident's needs.'

'Impossible!' scoffed Merkidon the Mummy, nearly blowing off his bandages. 'Your magic is powerful, I'll grant you. But not powerful enough to sustain that many properties at once.'

The group was inclined to agree.

'Ahem,' said Kirk, leaning into view of the webcam. 'Aren't you forgetting, Merkidon, that your sarcophagus was completely destroyed in last year's earthquake and that the only thing holding it together to this day is Helena's magic?'

'Well, yes, but—'

'And you, Cynthia,' Kirk continued, 'Are currently enjoying the clearest waters you've ever swum in, thanks to Helena's purification spells.'

'Yes, they're lovely, but—'

'And just how do you think they remain so pristine, despite you near-nightly entertaining those rowdy dolphins, hmm?'

This gave Cynthia pause for thought; the dolphins were a slapdash, sloppy bunch.

'And you, Transporto,' said Kirk, raising his wing. 'What do you suppose prevents you from popping away to Mars, or Jupiter—or heaven forbid, the Andromeda Galaxy, from which you may never return?'

'I… <*pop! … chzip!*> I guess I never thought of that.'

'It's because Helena uses her power to keep you here. To keep you safe. Half an hour every night before bed, she performs the necessary orbital chants. And that's on top of every other spell she performs for each of you, over and over again, some of which require constant concentration as she goes about her day.'

The Snitches looked at Helena with newfound respect. They had known she was kind; they had known she was selfless. But until now they'd been oblivious of the scale.

'That must be exhausting, Helena,' said Cynthia the Siren. 'Thank you, darling.'

All of them followed one after the other.

'Thank you, Helena.'

'Thank you, you beautiful thing.'

'Oh, bless my bandages, sweetheart.'

'Where would I be <*pop! ... chzip!*> without you?'

A tear rolled down Helena's cheek. She loved them all so much. She just wanted to help. That's all she'd ever wanted.

'There, there,' said Kirk, wrapping his warm talon around her little finger. 'You've always been a good egg. It's long past time everyone knew *how* good.'

She looked into his big, soulful eyes and couldn't help but smile. 'Oh, Kirk.'

The faces of her friends looked back at her warmly. She knew they supported her plan. She knew they would stand by her at every stage, no matter the setbacks. And most of all, with Darmon returning, she knew they were prepared to fight by her side—however they could—for the sake of those too weak to fight for themselves.

'Well,' said Kirk, wrapping his wing over Helena's shoulder and tilting his head into the webcam. 'Let's make some magical properties.'

The Snitches erupted with cheers.

POUNCING SHADOWS

A tale in black and white.

Being a cat and a detective ain't easy. You wake up one morning, expecting it to be sunny, and you find yourself lying face down in the gutter, one whisker past midnight. Time dances around, elusive, like a goldfish in a pond.

Nine lives? Hah. You ain't got more lives than any other animal. But folks don't buy that. They think the fairy tale's real. They try an' take you down a notch. Maybe five lives to four. Or four to three. They don't care if they might be takin' you down to zero. As long as they get the thrill.

That's what's wrong with this city. Too many hopped up bozos lookin' for a new high to make 'em feel alive. Well, I've got news for the lotta ya: As long as these paws are prowlin' the streets, you better keep your snouts low and your eyes wide open—cos this cat ain't the cuddlin' kind.

Four o'clock. Cap's got me pulling night shift again. Some kind of punishment for bringing Timmy Two-Feathers downtown without a warrant. Roughed him up real good in interrogation. Held his own, though. Not bad for a pelican. They usually break after the first five pool balls in the pouch. But not this bird. He's got too much to lose. I'm gonna have to find another way to make him sing.

Timmy Two-Feathers? Head of the Beak & Claw Gang. Smuggling narcotics, weapons and contraband in and outta the city. They've been gettin' away with it, too. The top brass has been taking bribes under the table for years. Turning a blind eye. Lettin' good folks get hurt. But that ain't happenin' for much longer. Not on my watch.

After losing a partner, you find yourself decidin' enough's enough.

An hour passes. I watch the same old riff-raff come and go. Drug pushers. Street whores. The desperate. The lonely. They congregate in the shadows, souls lit by the flicker of neon.

I see that old alligator, Jimmy Carmichael, dragging his tale through the gutter trash. He don't care no more. Lost his way after borrowin' cash from a loan shark down on Fifth. Takes a bite outta every soul that sets foot in its store. Don't matter how desperate, how vulnerable. It ain't got no conscience. Just a pair of dead black eyes and a taste for blood; smells it a mile away.

I hear the Gibbon Gang whooping and hollering. Always travelling by street lamp, never on the ground. Shifty bastards. No tellin' how many purses they've snatched tonight. By the smug look on their boss's rubber face, I'd say half a dozen.

Then there's Jane Reynolds. Leopardess from uptown. She comes down here twice a week to volunteer at the veteran's hospital. Paying her dues after a life of denial in the pursuit of riches. Former wife to the second biggest crime boss in town. Before he got stomped in his own restaurant by Tommy Trunk—you guessed it, an elephant with a grudge. Nowadays, she don't have two pennies to rub together. Alls she's got is her two diamond rings and a fluffy designer coat. But she won't pawn 'em. She's holdin' on to whatever shreds of dignity she can. And this city respects that. Not even the scummiest scumbags will try anything with her.

What did that author say? *A world of shadows bows to the light.*

And change? Well, this city's like a clock that ticks in two directions. One hand forward, another backward.

One day a wolf is making the same mistakes it always does: prowlin', stalking its prey, circling the streets lookin' for an easy kill; the next, it's helping an old rabbit cross the street. Crime and redemption, tickin' away in opposite directions.

Makes it hard to tell the time. But that's the way this city works. It don't ever really go forward. But it don't fall that far backward, either.

And me? Well, I've got plenty of sins. But I also got the scars that paid for 'em. Someone's gotta keep an eye on this town. And if that's gotta be me, so be it. I'll be doing it one night at a time until this tail don't wag no more.

The Swooping Sparrow. Timmy Two-Feathers's joint. Just a matter of time before someone shows up who don't belong here. Someone who stands out like a bulldog walkin' backwards.

I don't got no warrant. But I don't need one when justice is on my side. Soon as something fishy goes down, I'll be ready to pounce.

Another hour passes, and my eyelids are feeling heavy. Evie Jones is playin' on the radio. A fellow feline. Nice broad. Tough, too. Got stuck in a revolving door with her at the High Flyer's Hotel last Christmas. She didn't bat an eyelid.

Meanwhile, some dopey raccoon wearing a pinstripe suit in the next compartment was losing his cool.

Her voice reminds me of the sea. Think I'll retire there one day. Get me a little place where the water don't splash too high. Watch the sunsets. Purr a little. Maybe ask her over one night for a drink...

A Crimson Comet pulls up at the curb. '97 model, flames painted down the side. Tinted windows. Plates from outta town. Must be bringing in new muscle after what I did to their big-beaked bastard-boss.

Which means I got 'em right where I want 'em... Spooked.

Out steps a tall glass o'water. Posh from head to tail. Half-smile. Slippery skin. An iguana. Haven't seen one of them in years.

Then slithers out a bone-coloured anaconda. Bow tie. Top hat. Props itself up high. That takes skill. Most snakes go through life horizontal-like.

Finally, a beast in a blue suede suit. Make that a lion. Full mane. Broad shoulders. Packing heat by the shape of its belt. Turn around, you bastard. Lemme see your whiskers...

No... It can't be.

My old partner, Lionel Montgomery. The only big cat on the police force. Until he died in an explosion three years ago.

Or so we all thought.

Forensics didn't find a body. Just Lionel's lucky ring on a pile of ash. Been carrying it with me ever since.

Fireworks factory. Front for a weapons racket. We got the call to go in, hard. Lionel leapt up to the second floor. Damn, he was athletic. I did my best. Went the long way. Knocked out two goons in the stairwell. Took a hit to the ribs. Scratched a third goon 'till he couldn't see no more. Got a clear run to the second floor. Made it to the landing. A half-blink later, the whole joint goes up like the Fourth of July. Purple flashes and a wall of smoke. Then it was lights out.

Woke up in an ambulance. Tail fur burned black. Stayed that way ever since. Called out for Lionel. He never came. Died in the line of duty, Cap said. Flowers at the precinct. Memorial service. Obituary in the paper. Case closed.

But there he is. Wearing a suit made by Timmy Two-Feather's personal tailor. The pink stitches give it away. And the mane, all curled and blow-dried like a house cat. Standing tall, no regrets, no shame.

Makes me wanna cough up a fur ball.

That cat's got a helluva lot of explaining to do cos he just blew this case wide open. But this time, I ain't the one that's gonna get burnt.

Driving back to the precinct, I hear an ominous broadcast on the radio.

'And in breaking news, the head of the meteorological society has issued an urgent warning to all creatures in the city and coastal areas: from midnight tonight, stay inside. Close your windows. Block up the cracks beneath your doors. A cold front is moving in from the ocean. Cargo ships and sailors are already reporting capsized vessels and lives lost. We don't know the extent or cause of this weather event, but please: get ready for a turbulent evening, folks.'

Already one step ahead of you. My life just got turned upside down. My old pal, my closest buddy on the force, turns out to be a crook. Faked his own death and put me through hell just to make a profit. You think you know people. You think you can count on 'em. Share a bit of your life with 'em. Nah. Not me. Not anymore. Those days are gone. Now, I want to nail that two-faced bastard and burn his world to the ground. And I ain't waiting for the weather to clear. I'm going back tonight once I got me some real hardware. Something that'll send him running for his kitty litter.

'What the—'

Rounding the corner, my brakes fail. Slamming the pedal, but nothin's happening. The wheel shakes so hard on the gravel I lose my grip. The car smashes through the railing and over the cliff.

Fur stands up. Claws come out. Spinning so fast, I can't see nothing but a blur.

The sound of glass shattering. Branches snapping. Free fallin' again. Then *boom* and *splash*. Metal against the sea.

Broken windows. Water flooding in. My head hurts, can't move, tail tangled.

A photo of Lionel and me floats up from the glove compartment. The day we both made detective. The good old days…

I never liked the water. Always got under my fur. Never felt right.

Then again, *life* never felt right. Like the world was seeping in uninvited. Soggin' me out.

Maybe I was always falling from this cliff, hoping I'd land on all four feet.

Vision's gettin' dark. Guess this is the final scene. I'll never know what the hell happened—or why. But who cares, now? I could use some shut-eye.

Time for a cat nap…

It's been three months since the accident. Nurses fed me and stitched me up. Helped me walk again. Angels, the lotta them. Still hurts to bend down and clean my tail, but nothing a little purring can't solve. I don't hear too well out my right ear, but the doc says that'll clear up in time.

Time… Time's all I got now. Cap took my badge and gun. Gave me a severance package and said no hard feelings. Said it was for my own good. Says I was gettin' too close to the case.

Too close to tearing down their whole damned web of lies.

But they sure showed me. Cut my brakes. Left me for dead. Don't know how I'm still breathing, why they ain't finished the job. Maybe that big storm spooked 'em, like the voice of God. Or perhaps they think I got the message.

These clowns, they sure know how to make an old stray laugh. But the joke's on them. You don't trim these whiskers without getting scratched. And badge or not, these streets are mine; I walk 'em every night and know the back alleys. I know who's been where and the scent of the wind. I got friends in low places. Eyes in the shadows.

Nah. The fairy tale's true, fellas: you'll have to kill me another eight times before I get the damn message.

THE SEA CLIMBER

The following fragment was translated from a scroll entitled The Chronicles of Aerwold. Its vivid descriptions correspond to a mural painted on the ceiling of the cave where it was found.

The Sea Climber strode across the churning waters, his soul at one with the waves, his eyes fixed on the heart of the storm.

He sliced through the banshee-night winds, his feet sinking and rising—sliding yet never slipping—across the dark blue fins of seawater. His bones shook as bolts of lightning forked and thrust their way beneath the waves. The scent of panic sprayed his face as a pod of fifty whales sailed beneath his feet in the opposite direction, followed by an army of stingrays. Lighting the way was a flurry of firefish, whose orange glow was a moving lighthouse for all the lost and frightened watery folk. The Sea Climber felt each creature's fear and heard every voice crying out from the deep. They formed a deafening cacophony, masked only by the intermittent and vengeful slams of thunder overhead.

His heart pounded as he went deeper into the maelstrom. The wind was chaos and the sky was ice. An unnatural light, born in the deep, bled up through the waters and broke the surface, its radiance playing on the black clouds above—a pulsating, purple glow. The Sea Climber knew it could be only one thing: the *Skur,* a creature born at the death of the old world in the mutating fires of creation. And now, as was foretold, it rose from its thousand years of slumber.

The Sea Climber spun his left palm against the wind, calling upon the waters to ready themselves for battle. As he did, Aerwold—for that was his name—realised this would be the most treacherous beast his people had ever faced. No one from Galthar the Great to his glorious father, Reuyond the Tide Master, had fought a foe like Skur. And none of them had fought their greatest battles *alone*.

Ever since the plague destroyed Aerwold's people ten years earlier, he'd patrolled these coastlines alone, fulfilling his destiny as a Sea Climber. His sense of duty had kept him company on many a long, harrowing day. But this night, as Skur's jagged spine punctured the sea like a rising mountain, he felt utterly and helplessly alone.

Sensing the battle was mere moments away, Aerwold commanded the sea, and it rose—propelling him skyward on a hundred-foot spiral of water, flanked on all sides by swirling shields of sand and plume. He rode it on a sideways arc, gazing down at the monster from all angles, analysing its bone structure and searching for any weakness he could find. His people had known little about this beast, only that it was born from destruction and born to destroy.

He pulled his scimitar from its barnacled scabbard. The steel hummed to life, glistening with emerald light. It beat back the raging dark and liquefied the shards of icy rain. The sword of his fathers—fuelled and ferocious with the memories of a dozen generations—crackled with power. To his surprise, Aerwold heard voices within the steel—his ancestors whispering words of wisdom and courage. Half-smiling, he tightened his grip on the hilt, sensing the blade's desire to shoot forth of its own volition and sunder the beast below—the beast whose awakening had unsettled the currents and ignited the blood-magma of the sea. For days now, volcanoes had been erupting to the east, lighting up the horizon with flashes of red; tidal waves were carving clean the western coasts, razing cities and burying thousands in grim and watery graves.

Aerwold was the last of the Sea Climbers, the final ocean guardian. He knew that if he failed to destroy this foul titan, its malice would spread across the lands until every spark of life had been washed from existence. It was up to him, and him alone, to secure victory. To save all the good and innocent folk of sea and land alike. And he knew the secret to this victory lay in the first lesson his father had taught him. The first and most sacred lesson of the Sea Climbers…

Scholars from multiple worlds have been unable to discern the scroll's planet of origin or the parchment's age. Trace chemicals detected in the chronicler's ink reveal the presence of th'ar particles, a subatomic residue found on objects known to have travelled back in time by traversing the cords between galaxies (based on our meagre experiments to date).

The only other clues—though no less bewildering—are a sketch of what looks to be a bipedal creature with only two eyes and a short sequence of characters scribbled in the bottom corner: 3183 AD, EARTH.

LITERARY FRICTION

Nature abhors a bad novel.

Welcome to *Tree Talk;* I'm Juniper Flores.

Tonight we continue our series on neighbourhood pines, where we interview the oldest and wisest trees in our own back yards.

When *The Sound* passed over our planet three years ago it left a trail of mysteries in its wake, which are sure to keep our scientists busy for at least the next hundred years.

With strange messages carved upon the surface of the moon and the disappearance of the entire continent of Australia, one mystery leaves us feeling somewhat more hopeful than the others: those friendly new voices in our forests and gardens.

Like most of you, the first time I heard a plant speak—in my case, an azalea asking about my day—I nearly died of shock. But as the months went by and panic gave way to curiosity, we all found ourselves… in a gentler world; one where nature is finally able to speak for itself. The question is: how many of us are ready to listen?

Please enjoy tonight's interview with *Greenshadow*, a pine tree living in a small town outside Yellowstone National Park.

Juniper

So, Green-shadow. You were just telling me you want to be a writer. How exactly does a tree go about writing a book?

Green-shadow

Thank you for having me on your program. Well, first, I would want to know about my audience: are they connected to something like I am to the ground? Or are they free to move like a bird through the air? This is essential, for if they do not understand *connectedness*—how everything on Earth Mother relies on something other than itself—I fear they would not appreciate my stories. There would be a fundamental flaw in their assumptions, like explaining rain to someone who does not believe in gravity.

Juniper

What would you like to write about?

Green-shadow
I cannot see, so I have no observations to share. Although sight is not the only form of perception. I have felt the tremors of galloping hooves and the scrapes of gentle birds in my branches at night…

But what is night, other than coldness and moisture? You say it is dark to the eye, but I have no eyes. Darkness, to me, is merely the absence of warmth. What can be *seen* is meaningless, much like the thrilling sensation of sprouting a leaf is beyond your ability to experience.

Juniper
You strike me as a philosopher. Would you like to write a collection of essays?

Green-shadow
Yes, I think so. Fiction is a grand thing, of course, but what the world needs more than ever is truth.

Juniper
Many would argue that fiction is one of the best vehicles for truth.

Green-shadow
And I wouldn't disagree with that. But I would say that it is largely *inefficient* compared to a crisp and riveting essay. Especially those with a scientific bent.

Juniper
So, you have a scientific mind, too?

Green-shadow
In knowledge, philosophy takes us only so far; rigorous inquiry must inform our thinking. In so doing, our minds are opened to explore new branches of philosophy. They weave and climb together as vines upon the intellect.

Juniper
Do you read widely? Fiction and non-fiction?

Green-shadow
Yes. And poetry. I go through phases, but my evergreen favourite is *The Heart of the Tree* by Henry Cuyler Bunner. It shakes me to the roots. I wish I could meet the human who planted me on that crisp Autumn day forty-three years ago. I wish I could thank them. Sometimes I still feel nestled in the hollow of her hand. Her soul will forever be imprinted upon my own.

Juniper
Who are you reading now?

Green-shadow
H.P. Lovecraft. His style reminds me of the cold winter rains that trickle down my twigs.

Juniper
And how exactly do you read? Without eyes, I mean.

Green-shadow
I am connected to all books. We are made of the same stuff, after all... However, some have more pulp than others.

Juniper
And are you—

Green-shadow
—That was a joke. Though I don't blame you for missing it; my gardener says I have a dry wit.

Juniper
Are you bothered by the sacrifice necessary for humans to enjoy the printed word?

Green-shadow

I'm... *conflicted* over the issue: I value the spread of knowledge but grieve my kind's destruction. I mourn the death of any creature, actually, especially when it isn't *necessary*... Some of us cannot communicate as well as others, and some lack the confidence to speak up for our own survival. We trees are a shy, timid race; we're made to sprout, to grow, to live quietly and nourish our surroundings. It's not in our nature to argue. So, if I must die to have a valuable truth printed on my remains, I suppose that would be an honourable way to go.

Juniper

What if you became a trashy novel?

Green-shadow

I'd drag myself to the nearest shredder.

Juniper
Really?

Green-shadow
Of course.

Juniper
Well, it's just that—it seems a little harsh; after all, trashy novels bring pleasure to millions.

Green-shadow
Short-term, perhaps. But a lasting pleasure would be better, would it not? Something deep and abiding. Though I suppose we all need a little silliness in our lives from time to time... Very well: I promise not to shred myself.

Juniper
Which book has given you the longest-lasting pleasure?

Green-shadow

In my mind, the great writings all weave together into a rich world of truth. I am always there, even while I am here in a physical world of uncertainty.

Juniper

So, you've combined your favourite writings into a grand, unified story. A world that you can escape to within your mind.

Green-shadow

Yes, but I'm not the only one with this ability. We all have our own worlds to play in... I believe it was Aldous Huxley who wrote, 'Every man's memory is his private literature.' Let me adjust that to fit my hypothesis: 'Every man's literature is his private world.' I'm sure he wouldn't mind me saying that. Whatever the case, this I know to be true: the more we nourish ourselves with the writings we love, the richer our lives become.

Juniper
Green-shadow, I hope you know how much I've appreciated this experience. I'd like to think this exchange has played a role in bringing our species closer together.

Green-shadow
Consider yourself my new best bud.

Juniper
Wonderful! And I'm sure all my viewers will join me in wishing you a warm and vibrant Spring season. Thank you for your time.

Green-shadow
Pleasure.

HOW TO WIN FRIENDS AND SAVE THE WORLD

Step 1: wake up in a strange cave.

You know a gnome's in trouble when they wake up in a cave with no idea how they got there. When Fiddlebutton opened his eyes, he knew it, too.

He saw sharp stalactites hanging from a ceiling he didn't recognise. He smelled a strange fragrance unfamiliar to his well-travelled nose. He heard a moaning in the wind that made his knees tremble. Everything was new, and that frightened him.

He jumped up to run as fast as possible through the nearest exit. Gnomes are very quick on their feet, which is why wolves have such trouble catching them. But Fiddlebutton's legs froze in place when he saw four bodies lying in a circle around him.

'Oh my!' he gasped in a raspy voice. He clenched his tattered coat as questions flooded across his mind. *Who are they? Why are they here with me in a cave? Will they hurt me?*

The mystery of his situation had multiplied many times over. 'But even if they want to hurt me,' he whispered, 'at least I'm not alone.' He knew that was a silly thought, but he couldn't help feeling a little comforted by it. Being alone was his greatest fear, and as strange as this moment was, he was glad to have the company. Assuming this company was even alive.

He moved to check their pulses. First, a male elf whose slender arms were crossed gracefully upon his chest. Fiddlebutton marvelled at his long golden hair, which trailed across the watery grooves of limestone like vines down a wall. His pulse was strong.

Next, a half-orc. The gnome was always afraid to ask half-orcs what the other 'half' was. Lying on its big green face, its body bulging with muscles, the half-orc's pulse was *ferocious*. It snored as though it were angry at its own dreams. The frown upon its furrowed face revealed many scars from a painful past.

Turning around, the gnome looked down at the slender figure of a woman curled on her side. Judging by what he could see of her face, she was human; her nails were painted green, and her hair—the colour of oak—was decorated with little white flowers. As he pressed two fingers against her warm neck, he noticed a peaceful expression on her face. Whatever she was dreaming must be the opposite of the half-orc.

When he turned to check on the final body, he held back a scream. There lay before him a creature unlike any he'd seen—something frightening, dangerous and beautiful all at once.

It had elusive curves like a glamour-elf from the west, the jawline of a night-blade princess, and the willowy tail of a panther.

'It can't be,' he squeaked. 'A demoness!' His mind groped for answers and, ironically, took him to a place he thought wholly unreliable: a popular newspaper called *The Weekly Rumour,* famous for stoking fears about sinister creatures roaming the land of Antios. Fiddlebutton remembered an article about the "imminent return" of the Riddle Dragon (imminent now for over two hundred years). He remembered warnings of a curse that made one-hundredth of the population rise from the dead (still no confirmed sightings), and, most recently, he recalled a lamentation over the return of a 'secret race' known as *the demons*.

As the gnome regarded her deep, ocean-blue body, he realised that every detail from that *particular* story in that wretched newspaper was correct. Mesmerised, he carefully avoided the sharp spear tip of her tail and knelt down to check her pulse. Fingers shaking, he felt an unusual rhythm, much unlike the others. It ran fast, beating like a war drum, slowed like a winter stream, then rapid again—*boom ba-boom ba-boom ba-boom...* As he began to feel himself falling into a trance, he heard a gentle groan and saw a pair of fangs emerge between her sapphire lips.

Squealing, he tripped backwards and fell bottom-first onto the elf's chest. He expected a loud curse: *'How dare you?!'* But heard nothing. Looking down, he saw to his great relief that the elf was unstirred. 'Bless my britches,' he whispered.

Tentatively, he looked back at the demoness and saw that her fangs had disappeared. She, too, was fast asleep. He let out a sigh and removed himself from the elf. 'Oh, dear.' He held his head in his hands. He had only been awake for two minutes, and it had already been a *long* day. Here he was in a strange and scary cave with no memory of how he got there, surrounded by four strangers who could be anything from friendly to *fiendish*. He felt like crying.

'Come on, Fiddlebutton,' he said to himself. 'Remember what mother used to say.'

'RAAAR!' The half-orc's battle cry turned the gnome's blood to ice. The green beast sat up and lunged forward to strangle an enemy but was frustrated to find nothing but empty air. Fiddlebutton gazed in terror as the half-orc leapt to its feet with tremendous power, snarling with warlike intent. He beat his chest and sniffed for prey. As if the world was bending to the half-orc's rage, thunder clapped outside, and a blaze of lightning lashed the cave.

Fiddlebutton, unable to move, watched as the face of death turned slowly upon him.

'Where is Bellvar?!' he thundered, glaring wildly at the cave and the bodies around him. 'Who is gnome?!'

The gnome fumbled with his tattered sleeves. 'My name? Oh, yes, my name is Fiddlebutton. P-pleased to make your acquaintance. I think. Mhm, oh, dear.'

The half-orc, now standing full height, regarded the gnome with violent suspicion. 'Why you awake, but Bellvar not? Why Bellvar not awake and gnome not?'

'B-Bellvar? Um, m-may I ask, who is 'Bellvar'?'

The half-orc stomped on the ground and beat his chest. '*I* am Bellvar!'

Fiddlebutton scurried back at the noise and fell into a puddle. 'Oh, my wet bottom!'

Bellvar's rage was interrupted by a calm voice from a dark alcove. 'Indeed.'

Bellvar and Fiddlebutton, both startled, saw the elf leaning gracefully against the damp cave wall, draped with vines. Fiddlebutton hadn't even noticed him get up. In fact, even as he read his remarkable posture, he had to blink several times to ensure he was really there.

'Forgive me,' said the elf, stepping forward. 'We often forget our tendency to find nature's hiding places.'

Fiddlebutton loved the sound of the elf's voice. *Like a gentle stream*, he thought, before realising he better hurry up and respond. 'Oh, um, now *three* of us are awake,' he said nervously.

'Good,' said the elf, stepping into a shaft of moonlight. 'It's not just me who's wondering what happened and how we got here.' He regarded the gnome wisely, his slender frame still, but his mind keenly searching for an explanation.

Fiddlebutton took a moment to admire the elf's emerald eyes.

'I don't suppose,' said the elf, turning his gaze toward Bellvar, 'that you could lower your voice until we've determined we're actually alone.'

The half-orc's blood pressure began to pound. 'Stupid blind elf! Use your pretty eyes. Look! Just us!' He pointed at the human and the demoness, still lying unconscious in the middle of the cave.

The elf sighed and raised an eyebrow; he'd had much practice over the years expressing his superiority. 'Orc, I wasn't talking about *them*. For all you know, there could be a horde of goblins behind that door.'

Fiddlebutton and Bellvar turned to see, for the first time, a set of stairs leading to a wonky wooden door. Bellvar felt the feeling he hated the most. He felt stupid.

'Oh my!' gasped Fiddlebutton. 'I didn't even... well spotted, elf! Or should I call you...?' Fiddlebutton waited eagerly to hear the elf's name. He loved elves. He loved everyone, actually. If there was one thing you could count on with Fiddlebutton, it was that he was desperate to make friends whenever he could. He would never reach a number so big that he would have to say, *That's enough, no more friends for Fiddlebutton.*

As it was, he had no friends at all. He'd found it terribly difficult to make one ever since... Well, he didn't want to think about that now.

'You may call me Arrendar,' said the elf.

Fiddlebutton's eyes opened wide. As far as he was concerned, he'd just made his first friend in years. 'Pleased to meet you!' He rushed to the elf, whose elegant pose was thrown off balance by this surprise. 'I'm Fiddlebutton!' He held out his little hand. He hadn't stood this close to an elf for seventeen years. So exciting!

Arrendar, who rather disliked the idea of being touched by strangers, took Fiddlebutton's hand gingerly. 'Pleasure, gnome.'

'Oh, the pleasure's all mine!' Fiddlebutton grabbed Arrendar's hand with both his own and shook away with glee.

'Uhhg,' came a gentle groan from the floor. It was the human. Fiddlebutton's jaw popped open as he waited to hear her speak for the first time. He wondered if she would be a new friend, too. He noticed as she twisted onto her side that her neck bore the tattoo of a well-dressed lizard smoking a pipe. For a moment, he swore he could see the lizard exhaling and a wisp of inky smoke billowing about on her skin.

'Where am I?' she said. Her voice was soft without being weak.

Deliberately soft, Fiddlebutton thought. Like she could command an army if she wanted but chose not to.

'Who are you?!' barked Bellvar. 'Who are any of you?!'

'Orc,' began the elf, 'What did I tell you about—'

'*Half*-orc,' said Bellvar, shooting Arrendar a burning look. 'Half-orcs *nothing* like orcs.'

Arrendar knew little about either and concealed this rare bout of ignorance by looking away, feigning disinterest.

Bellvar smiled. 'Not so smart after all, elf.'

Fiddlebutton felt the tension in the air and couldn't stand another second. 'Fiddlebutton! A pleasure to meet you—my goodness, you're tall!' He grabbed Bellvar's monstrous green thumb and shook it excitedly. Then, rushing to the human, he helped her to her feet with a giggle until he was up on his tiptoes. 'Another friend!' he squealed, shaking her hand. 'A great day! A *confusing* day. But a great day.'

Soon, the elf, half-orc, human, and demoness (once she was awake) would embark on an adventure unlike anything they could imagine. Together, they would save a ghost trapped in ethereal chains, rescue ape-folk from a wicked winery, win the honour of a proud and noble race of eagle warriors, change the mind of a god, and destroy a golden-skulled sorcerer intent on drinking the soul of the world.

I could recount all these history-altering moments in vivid detail and describe the perils and wonders each of them faced, but all that matters now—and all that will ever matter to Fiddlebutton—is that he made the best friends of his life.

And they remained his friends for many long and joy-filled years until, with a smile on his wrinkly face, he closed his eyes one last time at a perfectly ripe old age.

I guess waking up in a strange cave isn't all that bad.

DON'T SHOOT THE MESSENGER—HE'S ALREADY DEAD

Unfortunately, only the punctuation of this message could be transmitted due to a paranormal power outage. We apologise for any inconvenience. To lodge a complaint, please contact your nearest supernatural service provider.

_____. _____, _____
__. ____, _____?
'_____,' _____. _____
___, _____-_____.
'_____,' ____.
'____, _____.' ____,
_____.
'_____!' _____. _____, _____
_____.

———————. '——————,' ———————. ———————. '—————: ———, '——————————,' —, ———————.

'——————?' ———————.

'——————. ——————————.'

'——————, ——————————?!'

'———!' ———. <*reconnecting...*>

But then, just as I saw my killer turn, I ——— ———, ———————. '——————— ———————,' ———————. ———————, — ———————; ———————————————
———————.

———————————, ———————.
———————————————. —
———————————————, —
———————, ———————
———, ———————————. ———
———————————. ———
———————————!

'———————————,' ———————
—.

'———————,' she said, grinning. 'No one can hear us in here. Not even your precious ——
————.'

———————————. ———
———————, ———————
————.

'————————————————,' I pleaded, my pulse growing weak. 'This is madness! You don't have to go through with this. We can ————————.'

'———, it's too late for that. Besides: your death will serve as a necessary sacrifice to my lord.' Her eyes darted madly around the room. 'He is almost here,' she whispered. 'I can feel him rising in another world. The Sea Climber will not prevail.'

I reached for my ————————————————.
————————————————————————, ——
————————————————. ————————
————————————————. ————————
————————————————, but it was hopeless. As my eyes grew dark, I ————————————————,
————————————.

So now, all I can do is send you this message from the realm of the dead. Not even the spirits of the dragons can help me.

Whoever you are, if you are reading this, please: find my killer. Stop her before she completes the ritual and opens the way for her master, the Riddle Dragon. His eyes are chaos and his words are destruction.

Her name is S———— ————————, and she's hiding out at —7 ———— Street, T————————. When you see her, hold out your hands and speak the phrase, *Ra———— M—kk—*, and the ritual will be annulled.

You have until midnight. The world is counting on you.

For ——'s sake.

STAY TUNED OR SUFFER THE CONSEQUENCES

Who knew radio could be this interesting?

We are *back*. Joining us now is the controversial—if you don't mind me saying—the very controversial Minister for Dragons, the Honourable Glimrock Sanderbane.'

Perched on the edge of the workbench at Danny's Autoshop, the radio played the afternoon drive time show. A dozen mechanics kept working their spanners and power tools, which clanged and whirred in echoes around the oil-scented garage. They half-listened to the confrontation that was about to unfold and half-dreamed about getting home to be with their families.

Outside, the orange sun began slowly melting across the horizon. About four-hundred-thousand other radios across the city and surrounding suburbs were tuned in for the hotly-anticipated face-off between *loud-mouthed radio personality* and *sly politician*. They all knew that the host, Bags Malone, was poised with an arsenal of combustible questions.

Bags continued his introduction, his tone shifting back and forth from stern to playful like a form of vocal jazz—always unpredictable but always compelling. 'The Minister has, well, gotten himself into some strife over the last couple of days for some of the things he's said in front of the cameras *and* in Parliament House. He's called goblins "a bunch of lazy dole bludgers," and just yesterday, he called—yes, you did, I'll come to you in a moment, Minister—he called wizards "a pack of shrewd mongrels." But to his credit, he's come on the show today to explain himself and provide a bit of clarity around these comments and some other controversies. So, without further adieu, ladies and gentlemen, please welcome the Minister for Dragons, Mr Glimrock Sanderbane.'

The pre-recorded sound of applause came over the radio, as it always did when Bags Malone introduced someone on the show. No matter how much Bags liked or disliked a guest—no matter how they differed politically—he treated everyone the same: they got the hard questions, but they also got the chance to tell their side of the story. Mostly.

'Well,' began the Minister, 'I'd say it's a pleasure to be here, but after that introduction, I'm not so sure.' He spoke in a tightly controlled tone as if his vocal cords were rusty cello strings.

'Oh, *don't* be like that,' Bags jumped in, 'you're here, you're on the show, and you'll get all the time in the world to defend yourself, which—oh, by the way, I just called you "Mr" by mistake, I should be calling you "Minister" shouldn't I?'

Glimrock Sanderbane, who was not only the longest-serving Member of Parliament but also one of the oldest dragons in the land, was very much a proponent of tradition and respect. His answer was clear: 'You know me well enough to know I like doing things the old-fashioned way— I'm not ashamed of that—'

'So it's *Minister*, then?'

'Yes, if you'd let me finish, I was just getting to that. I'd prefer it if you addressed me as *Minister;* not because I need affirmation or to stroke my ego or anything like that—'

'Thank goodness; we'd be here all night—'

'It's just—You're being insulting now, Bags, and I think it's in your best interests to show me, and your listeners, a little decorum, a little respect, and perhaps we can get this interview going forward with a *semblance* of dignity.'

'Well, Minister, I'm sure the good listeners of this program are used to the level of forthrightness and honesty they hear from me day to day; but I'm not sure they're ready for the level of doublespeak and *obfuscation* (he almost ate this word as he spoke it) that you're about to unleash upon them—'

'Bags, you're doing it again, and may I just say, you're treading on thin ice right now—'

'Thin ice? This is a free country, Minister. We have free speech, and if I want to speak my mind—'

'It *is* a free country, in large part due to my ancestors who fought off the Christmas Syndicate and their tyrannical invasion—'

'Yes,' cut in Bags, growing a little impatient, 'We're all aware of what happened, and it's enshrined in our nation's constitution. You even got your little Department of Deceased Dragons out of it. But that was three hundred years ago; times have moved on. I think the people of this country— the voters, the taxpayers—deserve some clarity on a few pearls of *stupidity* that've slipped out of your mouth of late—'

'I simply do not agree with the premise of your—'

'Hold on a second, Minister, just let me read these quotes out again, and you can respond to them.'

'Those are *mis*quotes, not quotes; they've been taken out of context by click-bait journalists who're desperate to keep their jobs and—'

'Just—you can respond in five seconds, Minister, don't get your knickers in a knot. Here we are with the first one. This is what you said on your way into the Crystal Fox Casino—goodness knows what you were doing there at 11:30pm on a Tuesday night—but you were asked what should happen to the gang of goblins that were apprehended earlier that night during a bank robbery. You said: "Don't get me started on that bunch of dole bludgers." '

'Exactly,' said the Minister. 'I said nothing about goblins in general; it wasn't a racist statement at all. It was clearly a remark—a somewhat careless remark, I'll grant you—about a specific group of goblins who had not only been caught robbing a bank but had, hours earlier, beaten an elderly unicorn within an inch of its life. So, in fact—'

'You're saying you were taken out of context—'

'SO IN FACT, I could have spoken much harsher words about those particular goblins, but it's not my *place* to comment on criminal matters; I'm not the Minister for Justice—that role, in fact, is being amply executed by my colleague, the

Honourable Clome Oddfeather, and he will no doubt take appropriate action in accordance with the relevant policy and legislation in a fully transparent and fair manner.'

'How long did you practice that line for, Minister?'

'Oh please, Bags, you're—if this is you at your best, I think you're over-hyping the level to which your listeners enjoy these broadcasts.'

'My listeners love this show; they've been—'

'How do you know?'

'We have a very thorough—Look, we're not here to talk about my show, we're here to talk about your statements—'

'And I've just answered your question about the first alleged slur. I've cleared that up for everybody. Now, do you want to give me the second one, and I can let the good listeners know how much of their time you've wasted with false innuendo and careless aspersions?'

'Well, I don't think anything I've done is careless—'

'Of course you don't; you're a *shock jock*. Everything you say is completely justified, I'm sure.'

'Okay, we—Jeez, let's get things back on track before this turns into a real schemozzle.'

'I think we finally agree on something.'

'Well, let's just clear up this other—you, *allegedly*, said that—'

'Here we go.'

'Minister. Did you or did you not say that wizards are "a bunch of shrewd mongrels"?'

'I said nothing of the sort. The hansard confirms what I said, the official transcript of parliamentary question time. I was asked—'

'We've checked the hansard.'

'Well, you've obviously not checked it very well because I've got a copy of it right here.'

'You've come prepared.'

'A dragon is always prepared, Bags, which I know causes you great consternation because you want all your guests to come on this show completely unprepared so you can flabbergast them with your—'

'I don't—'

'WITH YOUR ridiculous and, frankly, libellous questions—'

'How can a question be libellous, Minister?'

'How can—What?'

'A question. How can it be libellous? By definition, it's designed to seek information. It's not a statement. Only statements can be libellous.'

'Well, you've found your little loophole there, and I'm not surprised. Technically you're not committing libel by asking misleading questions, but the way I see it—'

'Maybe we should get the Attorney-General on the show, your old mate from university.'

'We did attend university together, yes—'

'And what a coincidence he got a top job in the Government just one year after you did, despite having no prior experience in politics or administration.'

'I resent the insinuation you're making, Bags. I have always prided myself on acting in the best interests of the people I serve—'

'That doesn't mean you won't bend some rules to help a mate.'

'Yes, it does. I would never act inappropriately to benefit a friend or colleague's career. You're treading on thin ice again, and I should warn you that—'

'There seems to be a lot of ice around you, Minister.'

'There is when careless people like yourself hurl careless remarks—or questions—whatever you want to call them. Just know that the more you question the integrity of your guests, the more you chip away at your own. Or what's left of it.'

A centaur police officer guided traffic through a bustling intersection on the other side of town. The lights had gone out for the third day in a row, but he didn't mind. It was part of the job. It put food on the table. Bought his wife that new dress for her birthday. Paid for the kids' excursion to the Northern Slopes. And him? All he needed was a whistle, a pocket radio, and some pep in his step.

'... now time to take some calls,' said Bags, returning from a commercial. 'How does that sound, Minister?'

'It sounds wonderful,' said the dragon, ensuring he sounded genuine.

'Good. We have Max on the line. Max, what's your question?'

'Hello, Max,' said the Minister warmly.

'Hello, am I on?' came a voice.

'Yes, you're on the air,' said Bags. 'What's your question?'

'Oh, uh—Minister. I was just wondering what the deal is with all these bloody basilisks slithering out of the sewers lately. They're turning up all over the place, covered in you-know-what, spreading their stink on everything. What are you lot doing to fix this?'

'That's an excellent question,' said Bags. 'What is the Minister for Dragons doing about this disgusting new pest? They can't speak, and they don't listen to police. They just go about the place wiping their filth over everything. What's the deal, Minister?'

'Well, to begin, basilisks do not fall under my portfolio responsibilities—'

'Now wait a second,' snapped Bags, 'Basilisks are a type of dragon. You are the Minister for Dragons. So tell me how they're not your responsibility.'

'It's simple. The *Reptile Act*, Section 9 Part B, clearly states that basilisks are not to be considered a relation of dragons because of "intellectual absence" and "the inability to exhibit honour."'

'Oh, you are joking.'

'No, I'm not joking, Bags. That is the legislation; that is how basilisks have been categorised for over twenty-five years. I know you're a little slow on the uptake regarding *facts*, and I'm sorry if you don't like it, but that's how it is. Now—'

'But—'

'NOW, in terms of their *behaviour*, yes: it's a menace. But this is being handled by a newly appointed task force, set up by the Government just last week. They're looking into this matter with some urgency, and the very best minds are on the job. So all I ask is that people steer clear of any basilisks they may encounter for the time being, and once a solution has been devised, we will deal with the issue promptly.'

'Okay, well, I'm not sure how helpful all that bureaucratic hogwash was to Max, but we'll move on to our next questioner. Dyad, you're on the air.'

'Oh, hello!' came a pair of female voices in unison. 'We were just wondering… Speaking as conjoined spirits, what is the Government doing about soul separation surgery? We've been stuck together for six years now, and we're still on a waiting list.'

The Minister spoke up before Bags could get another jab in. 'Thank you for your question, Dyad; it's greatly appreciated. Look, this isn't exactly under my purview, either. Still, I can tell you that my colleague, the Honourable Freda Dufflebag, Minister for Spiritual Affairs, is making a special evening announcement that touches upon this issue.'

'Well, what does that mean?' asked Bags.

'It means—well, I can't go into details as it's still Cabinet-in-confidence; but, Dyad, I think you will be very pleased with the Government's announcement tonight, so please tune into that broadcast, won't you?'

'Yes, we will,' came the voices. 'Thank you!'

'Well,' said Bags with a hint of disappointment, 'It sounds like you finally impressed someone, Minister.'

'Oh, Bags.'

'On to our next caller. Darmon, go ahead.'

The line was quiet for a moment but for the crackle of static. 'Minister,' came a voice, coarse and disturbing.

'Uh… Yes, it is I,' said Glimrock. 'Do you have a question for me?'

Again, a moment of silence prolonged the tension. 'Seventy-nine years,' said Darmon, bitterly. 'Seventy-nine years have I been stranded in your world. But the stench—I can stand it no longer.'

'I—' started Bags, a little unsettled. 'Are you saying you came through one of the portals?'

'Not by choice,' he spat. 'My enemies were still burning.'

'A-and… Why haven't you turned yourself in?'

Darmon sharply inhaled, and screamed: 'Black Fire!!'

Bags and Glimrock gasped in unison, caught off-guard by this sudden, frightening outburst. Those listening to the broadcast with a keen ear also heard a glass being knocked over and shattering on the studio floor. Meanwhile, Darmon began laughing euphorically.

'Now, listen,' said the Minister authoritatively, 'all portal-folk are required to turn themselves in to the authorities upon arrival. You have clearly learned to speak our language and use our technology, which means you know the rules and have decided to flout them.'

'You do not own the portals,' said Darmon, joyfully. 'You do not control them. You do not even understand them. Perhaps I was brought here for a reason. Perhaps it is your world I am meant to conquer.'

'What an *ab*solutely disgraceful—' said the Minister, until a high-pitched tone cut him off. People listening across the land covered their ears in pain until the sound finally subsided.

The voice of Darmon returned with a darkly triumphant edge. 'Fear not. I have found my escape.' The sound of wind and thunder boomed in the background. 'Consider yourselves… lucky.' The lights flickered all across the city and the earth trembled. Cries were heard from every quarter, and the sky twisted and churned with colours no eye had seen before. And then, after a terrifying moment—calm. An eerie, unsettling calm. Everything was back to normal.

'Well,' said Bags nervously. 'I—Thank goodness that's over.' For the first time in his career, he dropped the tough-guy persona. 'What do you think, Minister?'

Glimrock Sanderbane leaned forward in his chair. 'I think these are strange times, and we would all do well to pull together. These portals... They are our greatest challenge. They open at unexpected times and in unexpected places. Letting in all sorts of unknowns.'

'And so many of us have gone missing.'

'Yes, it's an enormous challenge, Bags. We all know someone who's lost a friend or family member to these vortexes. We don't know where they go. Our top scientists think perhaps they're spirited away to other dimensions, other worlds, other times. We simply have no way of knowing. And, most frightening of all—if I can be completely open with you and the listeners of your program—no one knows *why* this is happening. The patterns we're seeing indicate that it's unlikely to be a natural phenomenon. It's very possible that someone is orchestrating this for a reason.'

'Some have speculated it's the Riddle Dragon.'

'No, I don't subscribe to that theory.'

'But it's not as crazy as it sounds, Minister. Surely anything is possible with everything that's happened the past few years?'

'I—look, I understand where you're coming from, and I understand why people might consider this a viable explanation. But the Riddle Dragon's existence has never been proven. At best, it was a fairy tale—a frightening fairy tale—told to keep society in check by governments long past. But these are modern times, and I don't think we should put much stock in those old manipulations.'

'That's surprising, coming from you, Minister. I would've thought you held onto all the old traditions. Even the ones most people have cast aside over the years.'

'I do consider myself a traditionalist in most matters. But when it comes to the Riddle Dragon... let's just say I'd rather keep my options open to other possibilities.'

'Because that option would be too terrifying.'

'I didn't say that.'

'Well, that's what you're thinking, isn't it?'

The Minister took a moment. 'I've answered your question, Bags.'

Bags Malone, a veteran radio host, knew that his guest had not answered the question. But he also knew he didn't have to; everyone listening to the program would have heard what wasn't said and filled in the blanks. He knew everyone was afraid and that finding the balance between drama and comfort was his job. Too much of either would push his audience away.

'Let's move on and take some more questions from our callers.'

In a leafy western suburb, a wolf-boy climbed the steps to his home after a long day at school. The whole street was abuzz with speculation as people tried to make sense of the events of the past hour. On the bus, he overheard that dozens had died turning off their radios when Darmon's high-pitched frequency assaulted the airwaves. Police were refusing to describe the bodies in detail—saying only that they appeared 'drained', as if the life of each victim had been sucked out through their radios.

But the wolf-boy could only absorb so much bad news in a day. He had his own problems to deal with and they weren't going away with the next news cycle.

Reaching the door, he heard the radio through the front window, where his uncle would be snoring, surrounded by a sea of beer cans. As he stepped inside and dropped his hefty backpack on the floor, he let out a long sigh and entered the lounge room. Scooping the cans into a bag and covering his uncle with a blanket, he wondered if his life would ever really change once he graduated. Or, would he become just like his uncle, sad and defeated by some terrible turn of events—a burden to those he was supposed to help, a source of fear to those he was supposed to protect.

He wondered if any people listening to this stupid radio show were like him and felt trapped in a cycle of *mediocrity*—a word he'd learned only last year, which he liked very much. He wondered if they had family members who didn't know how to live life or let the past stay in the past. He pondered if anyone out there had been clever or brave enough to write their own destiny rather than let it be written for them by people less capable.

Maybe it was the dramatic events of the day, or maybe it was years of patience without reward (or a combination of both); either way, he found himself wandering over to the battery-operated radio—that damn radio he'd been subjected to all his life—and realised he had the power to make one small decision that might change everything.

He took the radio in his hand, walked over to his uncle, and threw it on the floor with all his might—shattering it into a dozen pieces.

His uncle sat up with a fright, groggy and wild-eyed. 'What the fuck?! You piece of—'

'You've met your quota for one lifetime,' said the wolf-boy, fearlessly. 'You don't get to treat people like garbage anymore.'

The wolf-boy's uncle glared at his nephew with bloodshot eyes. He wanted to leap off the couch and let fly with the back of his fists. It would be easy—he was twice as big. And besides, the boy was asking for it… But as the clock on the mantelpiece ticked away—*tick tick tick*—he found himself unable to move. His legs would not allow him to stand and he couldn't understand why.

You've met your quota for one lifetime… His nephew's words played over and over again in his mind. *You don't get to treat people like garbage anymore…*

He lost his grasp on time and found himself gazing at the floor. There among the old newspapers, bread crusts and burger wrappers, he saw the scattered pieces of the broken radio. He studied the shards of plastic, the twisted strands of metal, the snapped antenna—and then he realised: he was looking at himself.

It took all his willpower not to cry.

The wolf-boy quietly sat next to his uncle and scooped up a panel of wires and resistors. He ran his fingers along the edge as both he and his uncle remained otherwise still and silent for two whole minutes—until the silence was finally broken with a question.

'Do you think—' began his uncle, speaking softly for the first time in years. 'Do you think it can be repaired?'

The wolf-boy was more perceptive than most. 'I don't know,' he said, matter-of-factly. 'But if you're willing to try, so am I.'

Daniel Brewster

THE DEPARTMENT OF DECEASED DRAGONS

Thank you for reading *The Department of Deceased Dragons*.

If this tickled your brain, made you laugh, or put you in the hospital, please leave a short review online.

And tell your friends—why keep all the fun to yourself? :)

Daniel Brewster

ABOUT THE AUTHOR

Daniel Brewster grew up in an alternate reality in the late 1800s.

Born to a single mother of twenty-seven children, he received excellent grades at *Professor Alexander Chameleon's Magic Academy*, where he graduated with honours. Specialising in animal sorcery, his dream was to use his new powers for the good of the *forgotten creatures,* as he called them: rabbits, hamsters, beagles, guinea pigs. Those on whom society tested all manner of horrible chemicals and trapped in cages, unable to scurry away or even stand upright.

But finding an opportunity to help them wasn't easy. And few sympathised with his cause.

Over the next five years, Daniel worked at a hair salon where he styled society's most prestigious dragons.

Just when he thought his dream was dead, he caught the eye of Glimrock Sanderbane, the Minister overseeing the Department of Deceased Dragons. As an elder dragon, he followed the old ways and relied on humans as his personal assistants. After accidentally burning his last assistant to a crisp with a wayward sneeze, he urgently needed a replacement—and chose his blue-eyed barber.

This unexpected career change exposed Daniel to a frightening world of wonders. It revealed the ugly side of society, with all its pettiness and lies, greed and folly. It showed the harsh machinery of cause and effect, churning away beneath a thin facade of idealistic language and polished smiles. It taught him the nuances of political discourse and how to *get things done* in a world that didn't want to change.

After two years, Daniel ran for office in his own right and won the election in a landslide. Ever since, he's convinced nearly a fifth of the population to adopt the Philosophy of Kindness, a term he coined during his final election debate. Simply put, Daniel convinced them to remember the *forgotten creatures* and no longer take part in their suffering.

In his second term, during a freak portal-incident, Daniel was pulled into your universe, where he writes stories that remind him of home.

Don't miss out!

Sign up to receive emails whenever Daniel Brewster publishes a new book. There's no charge and no obligation.

www.books2read.com/danielbrewster

BOOKS 2 READ

Connecting independent readers to independent writers.

THE DEPARTMENT OF DECEASED DRAGONS

FAKING

CPSIA information can be obtained
at www.ICGtesting.com
Printed in the USA
LVHW020840221022
731316LV00007B/560